Based on the TV series *Nickelodeon Avatar: The Last Airbender*™ as seen on Nickelodeon®

ISBN-13: 978-0-545-00815-0
ISBN-10: 0-545-00815-8

12 11 10 9 8 7 6 5 4 3 2 1   7 8 9 10 11 12/0

Printed in the U.S.A.

First Scholastic printing, November 2007

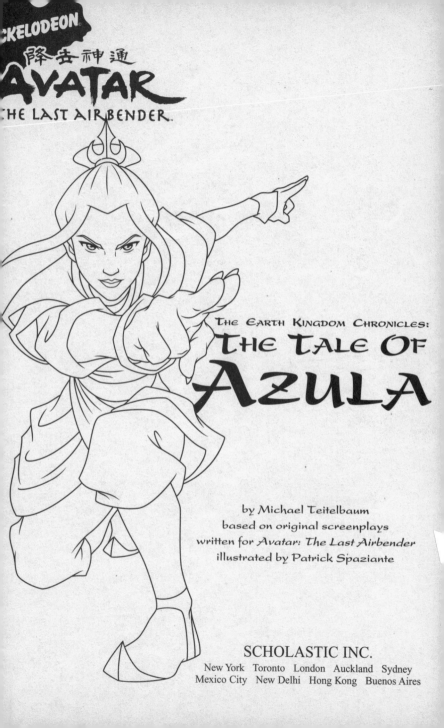

NICKELODEON

降去神通

AVATAR
THE LAST AIRBENDER.

THE EARTH KINGDOM CHRONICLES:
THE TALE OF
AZULA

by Michael Teitelbaum
based on original screenplays
written for *Avatar: The Last Airbender*
illustrated by Patrick Spaziante

SCHOLASTIC INC.
New York Toronto London Auckland Sydney
Mexico City New Delhi Hong Kong Buenos Aires

降世神通

Chapter 1

My name is Azula. I am a princess of the Fire Nation. My father is Fire Lord Ozai, leader of the most powerful nation on Earth. Soon he will rule all the nations—Fire, Earth, Water, and Air. They will fall under his iron grip once my work is complete. Then, in time, I will succeed my father to the throne of the Fire Nation and become the next Fire Lord.

But first things first. My task at the moment is to track down my uncle and my brother and return them to the Fire Lord for the punishment they deserve. My uncle Iroh is a traitor and a coward. Oh sure, once he was considered a great warrior, but when he ran from the battle of Ba Sing Se, he let control of the Earth Kingdom slip from his grasp. For that he has been banished from the Fire Nation for life.

And what of my beloved big brother, Zuko? He is a failure, total and complete. My father said so just recently when he assigned me this task. Of course I already knew: Zuko's been insufferable since we were children—a weak, whiny boy who never actually grew up. Whenever things didn't go his way, he would go crying to our mother—until one day she was no longer there to protect him. He would never stand up for himself, and he certainly never stood up to me. He's been afraid of me since I was nine years old, and that's just the way I like it. I'm fourteen now, and I could destroy him with just one look. And to think that he's next in line to become Fire Lord! The very idea makes me laugh.

I know Zuko's older than me. But Iroh is older than HIS brother, and Iroh's cowardice and incompetence rendered him unworthy of the throne. And so it was my father, Ozai, who became Fire Lord. Well, history has a strange way of repeating itself. I believe that once again the younger sibling will ascend to the throne of the Fire Nation when the time comes. I will be the next Fire Lord, definitely not my useless brother.

Zuko was banished from the Fire Nation for disrespecting our father. He has since been searching for the Avatar, to bring that little pest back to Father and eliminate any threat to the Fire Nation's plan for world domination. But, of course, Zuko has failed. Time and again the Avatar has slipped through his fingers, and Zuko now runs and hides in disgrace with our uncle. But he cannot run forever, and he certainly cannot run from me!

My father has supplied me with a beautiful ship, a Fire Nation royal sloop, to be precise—and I am nothing if not precise. The ship is filled with the luxuries befitting a princess, and is crewed by Fire Nation soldiers at my command. A great warrior and leader deserves nothing less.

As the magnificent ship approached the port where Iroh and Zuko had last been seen, I addressed the troops who gathered on deck.

"My brother and uncle have disgraced the Fire Lord and brought shame on all of us. I understand that you may have mixed feelings about attacking members of the royal family, but I assure you, if you hesitate in your duty to me and to your country, I will not hesitate to bring you down."

I can feel the fear spreading among them like a plague. Good. I like it when people are afraid of me. Frightened soldiers are obedient soldiers. They will obey my every wish, or they will know my wrath. Trust me. They don't want to know my wrath.

"Dismissed!"

As the troops hurried off to their posts, the ship's captain, a spineless little weasel, came scurrying up to me, muttering some gibberish about how the tides wouldn't allow him to bring the ship into port before nightfall.

I know just how to handle this poor excuse for a soldier. "I'm sorry, Captain," I said with extreme politeness, "but I do not know much about the tides. Can you explain something to me?"

"Of course, Your Highness."

Weakling. I'd love to get rid of him. But then who would steer the ship? "Do the tides command this ship?" I asked him.

"I'm afraid I don't understand."

Of course you don't. You have no idea how close you are to vanishing in a flash of blue flame. "You said the tides would not allow us to bring the ship in. So again I ask you: Do the tides command this ship?"

"No, Princess."

He seems to be catching on. Good. "And if I were to have you thrown overboard, would the tides think twice about smashing you against the rocky shore?"

"No, Princess."

I see the sweat bead on his forehead and his neck muscles tighten. He is afraid of me. "Well then, Captain, maybe you should worry less about the tides, who've already made up their mind about killing you, and worry more about me, who's still mulling it over."

At this point the nervous man won't even make eye contact with me. "I—I'll p—pull us in at once, Your Highness," he stammered, swallowing hard.

Smart man. I'll let you live. For today, anyway.

Once we docked I made my way to a resort where our intelligence indicated that Iroh and Zuko were hiding out. Ha! Do they really think they can hide from the Fire Lord, or from me?

10

As I approached their thatched hut on the beach, my stomach turned. Fugitives hiding out in luxury—how perfect.

I moved silently to the hut, then peered through its window. There was Iroh, beaming with pride over his worthless collection of seashells. This was the once great warrior of the Fire Nation? The "Dragon of the West"? What a joke!

And there was my sweet brother, throwing a temper tantrum because he had to carry his own bags. Poor little prince: so spoiled, so pitiful. But kind Azula has a surprise for you both.

"Hello, Brother; Uncle," I said, stepping into their hut.

"What are YOU doing here?" Zuko cried, moving swiftly into an attack pose.

My, my, what a brave warrior, ready to defend his vacation hut. But so rude! Zu-zu needs to be taught a lesson in manners. Zu-zu. He hates it when I call him that. "In MY country we exchange a pleasant 'hello' before asking questions," I said. "Have you become so uncivilized so soon, Zu-zu?"

"Don't call me that!"

So predictable, my brother.

"To what do we owe this honor?" Iroh asked coldly.

Zuko masked his fear with bluster, Iroh with his stoic manner. But I know they both fear me. As well they should. "Must be a family trait—both of you so quick to get to the point," I said. "I've come with a message from home: Zuko, Father's changed his mind. Family is suddenly very important to him. He's heard rumors of plans to overthrow him—treacherous plots."

I think Zuko is intrigued by my "news," but he's showing me nothing of what he feels.

This next bit should get him, though. "Family are the only ones you can really trust," I told him in my most sincere tone. "So what I've come to tell you is this: Father regrets your banishment. He wants you to come home."

I'm still not getting a reaction from Zuko. Is he trying hard to be brave, or is he just stupid?

"Did you hear me?" I asked impatiently. "You should be happy. Excited. Grateful. I just gave you great news!"

"I am sure your brother simply needs a moment to—"

"Don't interrupt, Uncle!" I snapped. "I still haven't heard my thank-you. I'm not a messenger. I didn't have to come all this way to deliver the good news."

Zuko's eyes are glazed over. I believe he heard me, but he looks as if he's stunned. I admit I must have caught him off guard, but—

"Father . . . regrets . . . he wants me back?"

Ah, there's the hope and relief I was looking for. The fish has taken the bait. Why did I even think this would be a difficult task?

He is clearly mine. Now I just have to finish playing my role. "I can see you need time to take this in," I said. "I'll come to call on you tomorrow. Good evening."

I left the hut and hurried back to my ship. There is much to be done to prepare for my dear brother's return. After all, it's not every day that the prince of the Fire Nation boards a ship heading home for a "hero's welcome"!

The next morning all was ready. I lined my soldiers up on deck. They have their orders, and each one had better follow them to the letter. I'm waiting in my quarters. Is it possible they won't show? I don't think Zuko can resist the idea that Father has forgiven him, but I can't be too sure just yet of what he will do.

At that moment, one of my soldiers knocked on the door to tell me that Zuko and Iroh were approaching the ship. I hurried up to the deck.

As Zuko and Iroh stepped onto the gangplank leading up to the ship, I flashed them a big smile. "Brother! Uncle! Welcome!"

They are here. This is all too easy. "I'm so glad you decided to come!"

As Zuko stepped onto the deck I gave him a big hug. Then I bowed oh-so-respectfully to Iroh. That's when the captain stepped up to me and asked if we were ready to depart.

"Set our course for home, Captain."

Once again Zuko's eyes glazed over, lost in dreams of his homecoming. "Home," he mumbled to himself.

The captain turned to his crew. "You heard the princess!" he shouted. "Raise the anchors! We're taking the prisoners home—" The captain suddenly stopped, realizing his mistake.

PRISONERS! You incompetent fool!

Iroh looked at me with daggers in his eyes. He didn't trust me from the start, and now he knows the truth. But Zuko is so in love with the idea of going home that he still hasn't realized the meaning of the captain's words.

The captain turned toward me, looking for understanding and forgiveness. "Your highness, I-I-"

But I ignored him. Right now I have a more

immediate situation to take care of.

"Run!" Iroh shouted. My uncle sent a few of my soldiers overboard with some Firebending.

But poor, deluded Zuko couldn't believe his little sister had betrayed him. He charged right at me, rage burning in his eyes. "You lied to me!" he shouted.

How can you be so naive, big brother? Always expecting people to behave the way you would like them to behave instead of looking at the world the way it really is. "Like I've never done that before," I said smugly.

He really should know me by now. Oh, he's so angry! He may actually get up the nerve to attack me.

And he did. Zuko threw all he had at me, unleashing a Firebending barrage. Impressive, but nothing I couldn't handle. He's far too emotional and unfocused. I easily sidestepped or blocked each of his feeble attacks. I saw no need to strike back . . . yet.

First I'll just have some fun.

"You know Father blames Iroh for the loss at the North Pole," I taunted.

Oh, Zuko is furious! How delightful! His feeble attacks amuse me, and I can't resist continuing. "And he considers you a miserable failure for not finding the Avatar."

That one's sending him over the edge! He's even trying to kick me, just like when we were little. And just as I was then, I'm faster and better than he is. I'd almost forgotten how much fun this is.

"Why would Father want you back home, except to lock you up where you can no longer embarrass him?" I said with a smile on my face.

16

Look at him, screaming with all his helpless fury. There! He's overextended himself. Time to end this little charade.

I struck him with a series of swift Firebending jabs, far too fast for him to defend himself. Then I drove him back to the deck, where he lay sprawled, powerless to stop me. Now I will end this with a blast of lightning!

But as I unleashed a powerful bolt of blue lightning, Iroh redirected the blast away from Zuko and the ship. The lightning bolt slammed into a nearby mountain. THOOM! The force of the blast caused the deck to explode into a thousand fragments, and sent me flying off the ship and into the water.

Iroh! I should have gotten rid of him immediately when I saw him yesterday. Father surely would not have mourned the loss of such a traitor and coward.

My soldiers dove from the burning ship to save me, but I did not require saving. "Forget about me, you fools," I told them. "I am perfectly capable of swimming to safety! Go stop Iroh and Zuko!"

But they were too late. By the time the soldiers swam back to the ship, my tiresome brother and uncle were gone. I have failed in my first attempt to capture them. But no matter. First my incompetent crew will pay dearly for this disaster, and then I will resume my search. I will bring those two back to Father. Of that I have no doubt—but perhaps I need a different strategy for my next step.

降去神通

Chapter 2

After returning to what was left of my ship, I ordered my soldiers to round up everyone who worked at the resort. I should destroy them all for giving Iroh and Zuko a safe place to hide, but I will hold off for now. They may come in handy, especially if I offer a little added incentive.

I created a poster with images of Iroh and Zuko. Then I stepped from the ship and addressed the gathered employees of the resort, holding the poster high above my head.

"Anyone who harbors these two traitors will face the wrath of the Fire Lord!" I announced, rattling the poster for extra effect.

The crowd let out a gasp. Good, just the kind of reaction I wanted. They fear me and they fear Father. It is now only a matter of time before the fugitives are firmly in my grasp.

I consulted with my advisers, two wise old women, Lo and Li. They sat in lotus positions on either side of me as I contemplated my next move.

"When tracking your brother and uncle, traveling with the royal procession may no longer be an option," Lo stated.

"It may no longer be wise," Li added.

"If you hope to keep the element of surprise," Lo and Li said together.

Wise words indeed. The pomp and grandeur of this huge ship, this royal procession with all its luxurious trappings, are my birthright. But in this case they may serve as an early warning signal to

Zuko and Iroh that I am close at hand. Two individuals traveling light will have stealth, secrecy, and speed on their side against all this dead weight.

If I want to catch my prey I must be agile and nimble. I must change my approach. I will leave all this behind. I need to enlist the help of a small, fast, elite team of operatives whom I trust completely. We will move swiftly and silently, and trap the fugitives when they least expect it.

It's time I visit some old friends and recruit them to this all-important task.

⊕ ⊕ ⊕

My first stop in the search for my team was a circus. I was looking for an old friend from childhood.

Ah, there she is. It's been years since I've seen her, but she looks the same. Slim, athletic, and full of energy. She is working as an acrobat in the circus. What a dreadful waste of her talent—it is a disgusting, unpleasant place. What could she possibly see in all this filth? But it doesn't really matter. The next phase of her life, in which she serves her nation and her Fire Lord, is about to begin. I am sure of it.

"Ty Lee, could that possibly be you?" I ask politely, knowing the answer.

She turned and looked right at me. "Azula!" Ty Lee exclaimed excitedly. Then she untwisted herself out of the pretzel—like pose she had been in, and bowed respectfully to me. Even though we are old friends, it is good that she knows her place—and that she realizes exactly who she is dealing with. "It's so good to see you, Azula!"

"Please don't let me interrupt your . . . whatever it is you're doing," I said, glad that she was so enthusiastic to see me. She will prove to be a valuable ally.

Ty Lee went back to her stretching as I wondered what she was doing here among the smelly animals and circus performers. She is, after all, the daughter of a nobleman, and she attended the Royal Fire Academy for Girls, just as I did. I'm certain her parents would not want her to end up in a horrid place like this.

"Ty Lee, I have a proposition for you," I said. "I'm hunting a traitor. You remember my old fuddy-duddy uncle, don't you?"

"Oh yeah, he was so funny!"

Funny! What could she possibly find funny about that pathetic old man? My face tightened.

Sensing my displeasure, Ty Lee quickly and nervously added, "I mean, what a shame he's become a traitor."

Good. She knows when she's crossed the line with me. "I would be honored if you would join me on my mission," I continued.

"Oh, I would love to, really," Ty Lee replied. "But the truth is, I'm really happy here. I love this life."

I was not expecting her to say this at all, but I don't show my surprise. Her mind will change soon enough. "Well, I wouldn't want you to give up the life you love just to please me," I said, knowing that she eventually would.

Ty Lee bowed. "Thank you, Azula," she said respectfully.

"Of course, before I leave, I'm going to catch your show," I said sweetly.

"Um, yeah, sure, of course," said Ty Lee, as a look of confusion crossed her face.

Later that evening I entered the circus tent for Ty Lee's performance. I was shown to a private area, and was seated in an elaborate chair that resembled a throne. Proper respect for the princess of the Fire Nation. I was pleased to see it.

The circus master came hurrying over to me and bowed. "We are deeply honored to have the Fire Lord's daughter at our humble circus. Please tell us if there is anything we can do to make the show more enjoyable."

"I will," I replied.

I watched Ty Lee perform with confidence, high up on a tightrope. With the palm of one hand planted on a board that was balanced on a cylinder, she lifted her body straight up, her toes pointing toward the top of the tent. It is good to know her remarkable skills have not dulled with time. If anything, they have improved. "Incredible!" I exclaimed to the circus master. "Do you think she'll fall?"

"Of course not," he replied, without taking his attention away from Ty Lee.

"Then wouldn't it make things more

interesting if you removed the net?"

He looked at me, obviously shocked by the suggestion. But I could see that this useless circus person would not dare to defy my will. I could up the ante a bit more. "I know! Set the net on fire."

He was too afraid to disagree. With a quick Firebending blast, he set the safety net ablaze. Ty Lee, the dear, kept her balance, but I could see the sweat bead on her forehead. I hope she's beginning to get my point—but perhaps I could make it a bit clearer. "What kind of dangerous animals do you have?"

"Well, Princess," he began, "our circus boasts the most exotic assortment of—"

"Release them all!" I commanded.

The expression of horror on the man's face was absolutely priceless! He bowed, then hurried away. A few seconds later a thundering herd of animals charged from the back of the tent. Ty Lee's tightrope shook. She teetered on the brink of disaster, but, trooper that she is, she kept her balance. I see more sweat than before. Excellent. Perhaps my point has been made. If not, I'll just have to endure another performance.

After the show I joined Ty Lee in her dressing room. She noticed me walking in, but did not acknowledge my presence. Her face revealed nothing, but I knew that she was afraid. She remained silent. It was up to me to draw a response.

"What an exquisite performance, Ty Lee," I said admiringly. "In fact, I've decided to stay in town. I can't wait to see how you'll top yourself tomorrow night."

That did it. She turned and faced me. "I'm sorry, Azula," she said, smiling. "Unfortunately there won't be a show tomorrow."

You are good, I told myself. All it took was a few minutes and a few simple suggestions. "Really?" I asked, trying to sound genuinely surprised.

"The universe is giving me strong hints that it's time for a career change," she replied sweetly. "I want to join you on your mission!"

That was nice and easy. The first piece of the puzzle has fallen into place, and now it's on to Omashu for the next step in my plan.

Ty Lee and I journeyed to Omashu, the former Earth Kingdom city that now belongs to the Fire Nation. We were there to see another childhood friend, Mai, who just happens to be the daughter of Omashu's Fire Nation governor.

We met in front of the governor's palace, where Mai greeted me with a formal bow. It is good to see that she, too, does not take our early friendship for granted, and that she is wise enough to show me the respect I deserve.

"PLEASE tell me that you're here to kill me," Mai said dramatically. "Omashu is the most boring place in the world."

Then we both laughed and hugged. I've always appreciated her sense of humor, along with her loyalty. "It's great to see you, Mai," I said.

"I thought you ran off and joined the circus, Ty Lee," Mai said. "You said it was your calling."

"Well, Azula called a little louder," Ty Lee replied.

Good girl. I see her loyalty is also beyond doubt. "I have a mission and I need you both,"

I told Mai. And without any hesitation, she responded, "Count me in!"

This was excellent. Mai didn't even need to hear what the mission was. I now have two underlings who will obey me without question, who will fight and give their lives for me if necessary. Iroh and Zuko are practically in my hands.

"Just get me out of this place," Mai added. "I'm DYING for some excitement."

Soon you will have more excitement than you can imagine, my friend. But I must take care of one small piece of business first.

I had Ty Lee and Mai wait outside while I visited the governor in his throne room. Mai briefed me on the recent happenings in Omashu, and I am not pleased. Granted, the former king of Omashu, Bumi, is now a prisoner since he surrendered the Fire Nation, but apparently her incompetent father has simply allowed most of the citizens to just walk out of the city. It's inconceivable to me how he could let that happen! Among them was his young son, who ended up in the hands of the resistance. And now the leaders of the resistance want to trade the former king for the governor's son.

"I apologize, Princess," the governor said. "You have come to Omashu at a difficult time. At noon we're making a trade with the resistance to get my son back."

You're trading a king—an Earth Kingdom leader—for a toddler? I hate sentimental drivel. "Yes, I'm sorry to hear about your son," I said, not feeling sorry at all. "But really, what did you expect by just letting all the citizens leave?"

"We thought there was a dangerous plague spreading," the governor replied. "We didn't know it was a trick."

I could not believe he was actually admitting how stupid he was! How did he become governor?

"My father has trusted you with this city and you're making a mess of things!" I snapped. "And in case you haven't heard, my father is not a very forgiving man!"

"Forgive me, Princess," the governor said nervously. "I CAN govern Omashu. I WILL do better. I just need a little time."

Time is a luxury you do not have. "You stay here. Mai will handle the hostage trade so you don't mess it up. And I will be by her side."

"Thank you, Princess."

Don't thank me too quickly. I will deal with you in due time.

Ty Lee, Mai, and I approached a wide plaza near the top of the city. Mai had handled the preparations for the return of King Bumi. All was ready.

A delegation of three resistance fighters approached us from the far end of the plaza: a short boy wearing a turban and carrying a staff, a girl, and a taller boy who carried the governor's child. I let a moment pass, then nodded for Mai to begin.

At a signal from Mai, a crane lowered a large metal cage from above. King Bumi peered wildly through a small window. This is the great Earth Kingdom king? He looks like a giggling lunatic who deserves to be locked up. Still, he is a king, and obviously of great importance to these people.

Mai stepped forward, as did the rebel with the turban.

"You brought my younger brother," she said.

"We're ready to trade," the boy replied.

Mai nodded. But something is not right about this. It's too easy, and we're giving up far too much. I refuse to let this happen. Still, this is Mai's little brother we're talking about. I must depend on her unwavering loyalty to me—which will now be tested for the first time.

I leaned toward Mai and spoke softly. "I'm sorry, but a thought just occurred to me. Do you mind?"

"Of course not, Princess Azula. What is it?"

The respect and fear is in her voice, and she addresses me by my formal title. This may not be much of a problem. "We're trading a two-year-old for a king," I explained. "A powerful Earthbending king at that. It just doesn't seem like a fair trade, does it?"

Now it's up to Mai. Will she agree with

me blindly, putting aside any feelings she has for her brother, or will this be the first conflict in our new alliance? She looked at me, expressionless, then glanced over at her brother, who was squirming in the arms of the taller boy. Then she looked back at me.

"You're right," she said. Then she raised her voice and called out, "The deal's off!" She signaled with her hand, and the crane lifted King Bumi's metal container back up into the air.

Excellent! You will be rewarded for your loyalty, my old friend.

"Whooooah!" King Bumi shouted as his cage rose skyward. "See you all later!"

The boy with the turban raced toward the crane. "Bumi, no!" he shouted.

So this resistance fighter has decided to be a hero. I will show him that he has made a grave error in judgment.

I unleashed a wall of blue flame blocking his way. But then something amazing happened: The boy leaped into the air, and his staff opened into an Airbender's glider! Then his turban blew off in the wind, revealing an arrow—shaped tattoo on his bald head. He is the Avatar!

Well, well, well. This IS my lucky day! It appears that I'm going to get much more than a toddler out of this deal. The taller boy and the girl had taken off with the little runt, but Mai and Ty Lee are sure to catch them.

Today I will succeed where my pathetic brother has failed so often. Today I will capture the Avatar!

The Avatar flew up and landed on Bumi's box. Then, using his breath, and what  appeared to be a form of Waterbending, he began freezing the metal chain that held it up.

But he will not complete this task. Using the pulley system that had lowered the cage, I hoisted myself up above the Avatar, then shot a burst of fire right at him.

No! My fire burst has only served to snap the chain and release Bumi's box, with the Avatar still on top of it. It's plummeting toward the city's mail chutes. Wait—my plan may succeed after all. When the container slams into that chute, both Bumi and the Avatar will be destroyed in one swift stroke!

Uh-oh. The Avatar has created some kind of air cushion to soften their landing. Clever. You are quite the challenge, Avatar.

I jumped into a cart used to carry mail along the chutes, and set off after them. I fired a blast, but the Avatar simply spun his staff, creating a whirlwind that redirected my fire burst.

Oh, this is taking much longer than necessary. I unleashed a barrage of fireballs one after another, but again the Avatar proved resourceful, outrunning or dodging my—

What's this? The Avatar has used his Airbending power to slice off the tops of the metal support beams above the mail chute! The beams have tumbled onto the track. I'm going to crash! I have to time this perfectly.

I leaped high into the air as my cart bounced through the rubble on the track. When it righted itself, I landed gently in the cart and continued my pursuit. Suddenly an enormous flying creature of some kind appeared out of nowhere. From the looks of it, it was a huge white bison. I have heard about Airbenders and their companion bison—this must belong to the Avatar. He's trying to make his escape. If he reaches the bison, I'll never catch up!

As I fired another burst of blue-hot flame, the Avatar lifted Bumi's box up off the track and soared toward the bison. Ah! He's overshot his target. They are flying right over the creature, and they're still in the chute.

I have to think fast. No one has ever resisted my fire-pinwheel attack, so I spun my hands swiftly, creating a rotating pinwheel of searing flames, then launched it at the container. This will put an end to—

Ahhh! A wall of rock rose up through the track, blocking my pinwheel blast. In a matter of seconds I'll crash right into the rock! I jumped out of the mail cart, which smashed into bits against the rock wall. Landing on the tracks, I could only watch helplessly, my fury growing, as Bumi and the Avatar escaped.

This boy is skillful and resourceful. But he has no idea with whom he is tangling. It is only a matter of time before he is mine.

I returned to the palace, where Ty Lee and Mai were waiting after chasing the other resistance fighters for a while. As we prepared to leave I explained our mission to them.

"So we're tracking down your brother and uncle, huh?" Mai asked.

Ty Lee couldn't resist the chance to tease Mai. "It'll be interesting to see Zuko again, won't it, Mai?"

They both laughed. When we were kids, Mai had a crush on Zuko. He may have felt the same way, but he was so busy brooding and sulking all the time there was no way to really tell.

I told the girls that our mission had changed somewhat. Though Father charged me with the task of bringing Zuko and Iroh back to him, I have now set my sights on a third target as well. Not only will I fulfill Father's wishes, but I will also deliver the biggest prize of all, the one that has eluded my brother: the Avatar!

降圣神通

Chapter 3

Tracking the Avatar is proving to be a more difficult task than I expected. His flying bison gives him an advantage, as he is free to travel anywhere without concern for roads, mountains, lakes, or other obstacles. We followed the Avatar through as much of the Earth Kingdom as we could cover, but soon lost him in the rugged terrain. I knew I needed a vehicle that could handle any environment I encountered. I acquired the finest all—terrain vehicle in the Fire Nation. It was a huge ironclad tank, with three sharp spikes that jutted out from the front. A tall smokestack belched black fumes from its top, and the thick treads of the tires were designed to travel over rock, sand, and water. The vehicle was even capable of climbing straight up the sides of mountains! Powered by fire itself, this tank could go forever without running out of fuel. Also traveling with us were three agile mongoose–dragons. We were more than ready for our pursuit of the Avatar.

We began our hunt and found that luck was on our side. A short distance from Omashu, we discovered several large clumps of thick, white fur leading in a straight line toward the mountains.

I recognize this fur. It is the fur of the Avatar's bison! Perhaps this is a sign, telling me that it won't be long before I stand before my father with the Avatar at my side.

Energized by this finding, I poured more fire into the tank's engine to increase our speed. With the city far behind us, we encountered a long, flat plain that stretched out for miles, leading to the mountains in the distance. There, in a wooded area at the edge of the plain, blue smoke curled into the sky.

I've found them!

I pushed the machine even harder, picking up speed. A short while later we reached the remains of a campsite at the edge of the woods. Charred cinders from a campfire that had been doused in water smoked and sizzled. Impressions in the grass showed where tents and bedrolls had been set up.

We are too late! They must have known we were coming and fled. But how? How could they know we were following them?

Then I noticed an odd tent, made from rock, jutting out of the earth. Is the Avatar now an Earthbender too? Or did one of his party do this? Perhaps whoever created this tent could sense the vibrations of our tank rumbling through the ground. I have heard that some Earthbenders can do that. But they cannot run forever, especially not from me.

We followed the trail of fur deeper into the woods. Our tank simply flattened smaller trees, while I steered around the larger ones. As we approached a clearing in the woods, there was a flash of movement. Several people rushed around in a panic, and then I saw them—the Avatar's bison rising into the sky, with four figures mounted on its back.

They headed deep into the mountains. The Avatar must think he can lose me, but he does not realize that his bison is leaving a convenient trail of fur. And of course, he has no idea what this Fire Nation tank is capable of.

We arrived at the base of a tall mountain, and then began to climb—straight up! We were amazed at how easily the tank did this. When we reached a plateau, there stood the Avatar and three others.

Apparently they were waiting for us— and ready to fight. Well, that's exactly what we were ready to do as well.

"Prepare the animals for battle!" I ordered. I shut down the tank's engine, and the tank rolled to a stop. Then Ty Lee, Mai, and I mounted the mongoose–dragons that had traveled with us. "Ready, girls? Now the fun begins!"

I threw open the door of the tank and we charged toward our enemies, riding the lizards hard. When we came to a river the creatures reared back, splashing across the water on their hind legs, their colorful necks flared wide open. Once back on solid ground, they dropped down to all fours and picked up speed.

Suddenly a jagged mound of rock sprang from the earth right in front of me. I tugged my reins hard to the left and skipped around the obstacle, but another quickly appeared before me. Again and again, rocks rose in my path, and in front of Ty Lee and Mai as well. However, mongoose-dragons are very swift and nimble creatures, and they were able to maneuver around each rock.

But who was responsible for creating these obstacles? I looked around as I pulled on the reins of my mongoose-dragon. That's when I saw a girl who had not been with the Avatar and his two companions at the exchange in Omashu. She stomped her foot on the ground, and a huge wall of rock exploded from the earth in front of me.

So the Avatar has found a skilled Earthbender to help him. Cute of him to think that I could be stopped by someone like her. But this is getting tiresome, and I don't plan on going around any more of these rocks. The time has come to go THROUGH them.

I fired a powerful Firebending blast that leveled the rock wall currently in front of me. Then the three of us raced forward.

Seeing this, the Avatar and his companions jumped onto his bison and flew off. The cowards didn't even bother to say good-bye.

We returned to our tank and continued to follow the trail of fur. It led to a clearing next to a river. Once again, we got out of the tank and surveyed the clearing on our mongoose-dragons.

I spotted a saddle and the remains of food supplies, signs that they had been here.

"The trail goes this way, Azula," Ty Lee announced.

Sure enough, a thick trail of white fur continued into the woods heading east. I looked at the river and noticed huge amounts of fur floating in the water. Then I glanced to the west and saw a wide swath of broken branches, leading in the opposite direction from the path of fur.

Why is there so much fur in the river? Of course! They must have finally realized that the beast is shedding, and that this is how we have been following them. They must have tried to wash off the creature's excess fur in the river so it would no longer leave an obvious path for us.

So then why is there a trail of fur leading away from the river to the east, when those broken branches show that the beast went the other way? Ah, someone must be using his brain, but he doesn't know who he's dealing with.

"The Avatar is trying to give us the slip," I told the girls.

Obviously, some of his group went in one direction, while others left some fur to give me the impression that they had gone the other way. I see that some of the fur along the eastern path is clinging to high branches. That means it was dropped from the air. If the beast went west, then the only one who could have flown east to drop the fur and mislead us was the Avatar himself—I had seen him fly on his glider back at Omashu.

This called for a change in plans.

"Ty Lee, Mai, you two head west, in the direction of those broken branches, and keep your eye out for the bison," I said. "I'm certain it went that way. I will follow this trail to the east, where I am sure I will find the Avatar!"

🏵 🏵 🏵

As my girls took off on their mongoose-dragons along the trail heading west, I rode mine heading east. How noble of the Avatar, willing to lead me away from the others to protect his friends, at the cost of his own freedom. And how foolish, too.

After following the trail for most of the day, I came to a deserted town. The sun was low in the sky and cast long shadows onto the abandoned buildings. There, in the center of the empty town, stood the Avatar, alone. I dismounted and walked toward him slowly.

He's smaller than he first appeared when he ran from me in Omashu. Brave Avatar, we shall soon see what you are made of.

"All right, you've caught up with me," he said boldly. "Now, who are you, and what do you want?" he asked.

I find it amusing that he tries to sound so tough, but he has the voice of a child! He has no idea who I am. I'll have to give him a little help. "You mean you haven't guessed? You don't see the family resemblance? Here's a hint."

I covered my left eye with one hand, then spoke in a low, raspy voice. "I must find the Avatar to restore my honor."

But there was no reaction. Boys can be so pigheaded about trying to maintain a tough exterior. "It's okay. You can laugh. It's funny," I said.

But he didn't laugh. He was no fun at all. Instead he asked seriously, "So now what?"

Fine. Be that way. I can play the serious warrior better than you. "Now it's over," I replied. "You're tired, and you have no place to go. You can run, but you know I'll catch you."

I didn't think he could look any more serious than he already did, but he narrowed his eyes and stared right at me. "I'm not running," he declared.

Very well. Let's just get to the point. "Do you really want to fight me?" I asked.

"Yes, I really do," replied a low, raspy voice from behind me.

"Zuko!" the Avatar cried, as shocked to see my brother as I was.

Well, well, well. A lovely little family reunion. Nice work, Zu-zu. I truly did not know that you have been following me. And I thought I'd have to track you down once I captured the Avatar. But now you have saved me the trouble. "I was wondering when you'd show up, Zu-zu."

The Avatar giggled. "Zu-zu?"

Of course this really annoyed my sensitive big brother. Zuko turned to me, his fists clenched, his eyes fierce.

"Back off, Azula," he said. "The Avatar is mine."

Oh, brother of mine, haven't you learned that I don't take orders from you—and I don't intend to start? "I'm not going anywhere, Zuko," I said.

The Avatar began sneaking away as though he thought he could take advantage of the conflict between Zuko and me. He is underestimating us. I immediately turned to face him and assumed a combat stance. Zuko did the same.

I can sense the Avatar's nervous energy. He's not sure who will attack him first or whether we will team up against him. Zuko is also fidgety. He's trying to hide it, but I know too well that he taps his leg nervously when he is worried. He has done this ever since we were kids.

I now have the unexpected opportunity to confront Zuko and the Avatar together. But who shall I deal with first? I have to make a choice.

I fired at Zuko, knocking him down. He returned a fireball as the Avatar tried to fly away. I dodged Zuko's strike while blasting the Avatar out of the air. He came instantly crashing back to the ground.

For a moment, Zuko and I teamed up against the Avatar, but I took advantage of our temporary alliance to once again attack Zuko. The strategic options presented in a three—way battle are quite intriguing. Still, I must remain alert to the movements of both of my opponents.

Zuko and I both hurled an enormous fire blast at the Avatar, but he flew into a nearby abandoned building, soaring up into the rafters. Zuko and I followed him into the building and discovered him floating on an air sphere. I shot a bolt of lightning at him, and as the sphere dissolved, the Avatar leaped to safety.

I will torch the entire town if I have to, but these two will not escape! I turned my attention back to Zuko for a moment. The force of my fire blast knocked Zuko out into the street. Then I turned back to the Avatar.

He ran into another building. I fired burst after burst of fire, which sliced pieces of the building away bit by bit. I now had the Avatar trapped.

I took a moment to savor the victory. The Avatar is mine. Nothing can change that! I sauntered into what was left of the building, and started a blaze that raced toward the Avatar. The look of terror on his face was priceless!

Seeking to prolong the moment, I drew back my hand slowly, preparing to unleash the final blow. Suddenly a thin stream of water slapped my hand down. Then the same water whip lifted the debris off the Avatar and released him!

Who dares to interfere with me?

"Katara!" the Avatar shouted.

I turned around in time to see a girl running from the building. Ah, she had been at Omashu with the Avatar. Well, this Waterbender will feel my wrath too!

I dashed after the girl, but the tall boy who travels with them also surprised me, attacking me with a boomerang. I stumbled backward.

But even working together, the Airbender, the Waterbender, and the boy with the boomerang posed little problem. I quickly regained my footing, then returned fierce fire of my own. That's when the ground began to shake violently, knocking me off my feet. This time I landed facedown in the dirt.

"I thought you guys could use a little help," said a voice from behind me. I scrambled to my feet and spun around.

The Earthbender! She has joined our little party. And she is not the only one. Iroh is here too! I knew that wherever Zu-zu was, Iroh would not be far behind.

"Uncle!" Zuko cried, sprawled on the ground.

"Get up," Iroh said, helping Zuko to his feet.

Let's see now, six against one. Overwhelming odds. I almost feel sorry for all of them. I feel as if my senses are heightened by this challenge. Attacks came from all directions — Earthbending, Airbending, Waterbending, and Firebending. I dodged them all, returning fire of my own with raging fury.

Then the group started closing in on me. Glancing over my shoulder, I saw that they were backing me toward a wall. Hmm . . . this will require just the right move at precisely the right time. But first I must distract them.

"Well, look at this," I said. "Enemies and traitors all working together. I'm done. I know when I'm beaten. You got me. A princess surrenders with honor."

I began to bow slightly, then quickly straightened up and blasted Iroh in the chest with my most powerful lightning strike. Down he went. Then the others reacted precisely as I knew they would.

The Airbender, Waterbender, Earthbender, my brother the Firebender, and even the boomerang boy all sent attacks flying toward me at the same moment. I easily danced out of the way, but the force of their combined blows sent up a huge explosion, blasting a hole in the wall behind me and filling the area with smoke and dust. It was the perfect cover for my escape!

I quietly slipped back to my mongoose-dragon and rode back toward the river. I wanted to find Ty Lee and Mai to plan our next move . . . but as it turned out, our next move came and found us.

降击神通

Chapter 4

The city of Ba Sing Se is the capital of the Earth Kingdom. It is where the Earth Kingdom ruler lives, and is the center of culture, education, finance, and agriculture as well.

My father and uncle knew that if Ba Sing Se fell, the Earth Kingdom would fall. If the Earth Kingdom falls, the Fire Nation will complete its destiny and control the entire world. Ba Sing Se is the key. Iroh tried years back to invade the walled fortress, but failed miserably. He didn't take the

Earthbenders' defenses and their resolve seriously enough, and it cost him dearly.

Since Iroh's failure, my father has been obsessed with taking Ba Sing Se. His war minister and generals have been working for years on a device to break through Ba Sing Se's fortified outer wall—an enormous drill. When I learned the drill was completed and on its way to the city, I knew that this would be the means to make up for my recent difficulties in capturing Iroh, Zuko, and the Avatar.

How sweet that I will be the one who finally completes the capture of Ba Sing Se. I will take command of the drill and lead the Fire Nation to victory. I will deliver the crushing blow that takes down the city and destroys the Earth Kingdom in one powerful assault. Once Ba Sing Se is in my hands, all else will become irrelevant. The Earth Kingdom will be ours, and the war will be over quickly— with my father in his rightful position as ruler of the entire world.

Mai, Ty Lee, and I caught up to the drill a short distance from Ba Sing Se. I immediately took command from the war minister, who had been leading the attack. He boasted that the drill would easily break through the outer wall of Ba Sing Se in a single day. Then he showed me the device.

The drill stood one hundred feet tall and was actually made up of two parts. The drill itself, which would bore an opening in the wall, was completely encased in a metal shell. The drill was connected to the shell by a series of braces, and the shell was impervious to any known substance or force.

I am thrilled! The drill is an incredibly efficient tool encased in armor that cannot be pierced. This machine is virtually unstoppable, and with it I shall begin the final phase of the Fire Nation's world victory!

I continued toward Ba Sing Se. The war minister remained with me and my crew, who ran the enormous contraption.

My father had also sent a fleet of small tanks to accompany the drill, in case we met any resistance. I laughed as I peered from the drill's command bridge at the tiny tanks, which looked like children's playthings flanking us on either side.

The view from the command bridge spread out before me as we approached the city. At my first glimpse of our target—the outer wall—the thrill of conflict swept through my bones. I live for conquest and success, and this time I will not fail my father.

"This drill is a feat of scientific ingenuity and raw destructive power," the war minister said as the wall drew closer.

He certainly does love his mechanical monstrosity. But his boasting grows tiresome.

"Yes, so you've said," I responded.

"Once it tunnels through the wall, the troops accompanying us in the tanks will storm the city. The Earth Kingdom will finally fall, and you can claim Ba Sing Se in the name of your father. Nothing can stop us," the war minister continued.

Ty Lee leaned over my shoulder and peered out the window. "What about those guys down there?" she asked.

I followed her gaze and spotted a platoon of Earthbenders lining up in the path of the drill.

within the cloud? I can't imagine it could be something that would pose a serious threat to this machine.

"Don't worry, Princess," the war minister said smugly. "I'm sure it's nothing. Just a harmless cloud of dust."

A few seconds later the cloud vanished, as if the drill had run right over it.

Maybe he was right. Perhaps it was simply a harmless dust cloud. Some trick of the wind. We continued forward, unhampered.

Suddenly the entire machine began to vibrate and hum. We shook and bounced for a few seconds, and then a high-pitched whirring sound cut through the dull din of the vehicle's motor.

We are in! The drill has hit the wall and begun its work, boring its way into the city. The assault on Ba Sing Se is under way at last!

"Congratulations, crew!" the war minister shouted into a metal pipe that served as the drill's communication system. "You can start the countdown to victory!"

However, a few minutes later the war minister's declaration proved to be premature. A bell rang, indicating an incoming message for the war minister on the communication system. In a panicked voice, a crew member informed us that an engineer had been ambushed, his plans for the drill had been stolen, and one of the braces that held the outer shell to the drill had been cut.

Sabotage! Somehow, someone has gotten into the drill and is trying to stop us from the inside! So that harmless cloud of dust was not quite so harmless after all. We must stop this threat before it spreads.

"Ladies, come with me!" I commanded, not even bothering to look at the war minister. I will deal with him after I finish handling this fiasco, for which I'm willing to bet my throne that the Avatar is responsible.

Ty Lee, Mai, and I hurried to the section of the machine between the drill and the outer shell. There, as I expected, we found the Avatar and his companions attempting to destroy another brace.

Very clev, Avatar. You may have snuck in here idden by a dusty cloud, but you will never ave this drill alive! You have interfered with ny plans for the last time.

I hurled a szling blast of blue fire at the Avatar, but h and two others dodged my attack. Then thy split up. The Waterbending girl and the er boy ran one way, the Avatar in the oposite direction. I did not see the Earthbend girl with them.

"Follow the I shouted to Ty Lee and Mai. "The Av is mine!"

The Avatar ppeared around a bend. I followed up chamber and emerged outside to find h 'terbending slashes into the metal armor top of the drill.

I unleashed a f flames at the Avatar, but he spun, and my attack aside with his Airbending. as also ready for my next attack, cou it with a huge gust of wind that swept d me.

You are goo vatar. But not good enough!

I launched m over his airburst and landed beside hi hen I fired a swift series

59

of short fire bursts one after another. But the Avatar slapped my hands aside with a whip made of water.

Impressive. His Waterbending skills have grown. But as everyone knows, fire evaporates water.

I focused my next blast right at his water whip. The whip sizzled into steam and vanished into the air. Just then, a flurry of rocks swept up from below, pelting both of us.

Earthbenders were attacking from the ground!

The Avatar redirected all the rocks at me, and I planted myself facedown on the surface of the shell to avoid them. After the rocks had passed me, I snapped back to my feet and blasted more fire at the Avatar. But he quickly formed more rocks into a wall, which deflected my flames. So he does have Earthbending skills as well now.

Thrusting each hand forward, the Avatar punched rocks at me. But I have come across attacks of this nature before. I drew myself up into the crane stance.

Balancing all my weight on one leg, I kicked the incoming rocks away with the shin guard on my raised leg, all the time moving closer to the Avatar and tossing fire at him.

Unable to counter my relentless onslaught, he moved backward, toward the drill.

There was nowhere for him to run! But I had no time to gloat. The Avatar suddenly drew loose rocks to him and formed a shield around his arm. He swung his rock gauntlet quickly and struck me in the stomach. Reeling backward, I spun around before regaining my footing. Just as I turned to charge at the Avatar, he was gone!

I looked all around the drill, but saw no sight of him. Then I looked up to see him running straight down the outer wall of the city. He could not be an easier target.

But as I drew back my hands, preparing to destroy him, the Avatar shocked me. He leaped from the wall, grasping a large pointed stone. He plunged downward, heading right for the slashes he had made in the top of the drill's armor.

I timed my blast perfectly. It struck the spot

where the Avatar landed—just as he drove the pointed rock into the shell. The armor tore open and the force of the Avatar's blow deflected my fire blast. Then a torrent of slurry, that sloppy mixture of pulverized rock and water that the drill funnels away as it digs deeper into the wall, slammed into me. Try as I might, I could not keep my footing on the slick metal surface, and the slurry knocked me from the drill.

No! I will not let the Avatar slip from my grasp again. Not when I'm so close!

And then it got even worse. I watched in horror as the entire drill vehicle collapsed, the braces having been split by the Avatar and his ragtag band. The weight of the outer shell buckled, then fell onto the drill mechanism itself, stopping the machine in its tracks. When I looked up, the Avatar had escaped again.

Then the back end of the drill opened and a gush of slurry poured out, depositing Mai and Ty Lee at my feet.

Mai looked up at me, stating the obvious: "We lost."

I was so angry I could barely respond. How much more time did I have to waste on the capture of the Avatar? It was clear that I needed to come up with another strategy.

Chapter 5

I need time to think, to plan. We failed at Ba Sing Se, and I have no intention of returning to the Fire Nation with news of another failure. My father gave me far more leeway than he ever gave Zuko, but he is not a patient man.

I left Ba Sing Se feeling a little depressed, but immediately felt better when, while traveling through the Earth Kingdom, we came upon more of the fur from the Avatar's beast.

Odd that the bison is so far from Ba Sing

Se—it must be separated from the Avatar. All at once I feel inspired. We will finally get the Avatar, and I will not have to waste any energy seeking him out: If I can capture his beast, the Avatar will come to me.

We followed the trail of bison fur into a thickly wooded area. It led us to a forest stream, where we eventually came upon three girls dressed in bright, colorful ceremonial costumes, standing in the stream bathing the Avatar's bison.

This search couldn't have been any easier! I fired a bolt of lightning to announce our arrival. It split a tree and startled the girls. The bison growled and snarled, but I could smell its fear. I waved a handful of its fur in the air. "My, my, you're easy to find," I said. "It's really astounding that my brother hasn't captured you yet."

The beast roared as the girls struck warrior poses—with fans! "Who are you, the Avatar's fan girls?" I asked.

"If you're looking for the Avatar, you're out of luck," one of them said.

"That's okay, any friend of the Avatar

is an enemy of mine," I replied as I fired a flaming blast at the girl, but the bison slammed the water with his tail, sending up a huge wave that extinguished the fire before it reached her.

While Mai and Ty Lee fought the other two girls, I launched a series of fiery attacks at the beast, and this time I could see fear in his eyes.

"Afraid of fire, I see. That's good, you should be," I said, before creating a ring of fire around him. Now the bison was truly terrified.

But one of the warriors doused the fire with mud from the stream. Now the animal had a way out.

"Go, Appa!" she shouted to the bison. "Get out of here! You have to find Aang. We'll be okay!" The beast took to the sky.

I turned my attention to this warrior, and knocked her off her feet with a leg sweep. I learned that these girls were warriors from Kyoshi Island—and quickly a plan took shape in my mind.

Ty Lee, Mai, and I returned to Ba Sing Se dressed as Kyoshi warriors. I was amazed at the warm reception we were given. The guards at the outer wall threw open the gates and welcomed us. An elaborately woven carpet was rolled out leading up to the palace. It was a little infuriating that Kyoshi warriors would garner such a welcome, but I will not complain just yet.

It's strange to think that all along I had only thought in terms of bigger and better weapons, of more complicated schemes to capture the Avatar. Yet all it takes is the right dress and makeup to open the door to the throne of the Earth Kingdom. And when all is said and done, that's exactly where I'll be seated.

The fancy carpet led directly to the king's throne. He stood as we approached. We paused before him and bowed respectfully.

"In our hour of need, it is with the highest honor that I welcome our esteemed allies, the Kyoshi warriors!" he announced to rousing cheers and applause from the gathered throng.

I bowed again and spoke softly. "We are

the Earth King's humble servants."

Following a formal welcoming ceremony, we joined the king in his throne room. There, he filled us in on the latest goings-on in Ba Sing Se. "It's been a difficult week. My most trusted adviser, Long Feng, and his Dai Li agents tried to take control of Ba Sing Se from me."

Tried? I believe we will have more luck than they did. "It's terrible when you can't trust the people who are closest to you," I said politely.

"But there is good news," added the king. "The Council of Generals is meeting to plan an invasion of the Fire Nation this summer—on the day of a solar eclipse, when Firebenders are at their weakest!"

Ah, that's their plan! All Firebenders dread the Day of Black Sun. It only comes every few years, but its effects are devastating. And while this news is shocking, I do not allow it to change my expression. Stupid Earthbenders; their plan will never come to pass—now that I am aware of their intentions.

The king has also foolishly told me all I need to know in order to successfully overthrow him. The key is the Dai Li. They are the elite members of an agency that keeps order in Ba Sing Se. I will gain control of them and set up a coup from within. And the delicious part is that the king won't even know who is taking over his throne!

Silly Earth King, you have handed the Fire Nation the ammunition it needs for its final victory. I must avoid eye contact with Mai and Ty Lee. They wear their emotions on their faces more overtly than I do. And I can't risk having the king suspect anything.

"Really? Now that sounds like a fascinating and brilliant plan," I replied with a smile.

We were led to the palace's most beautiful guest chambers, where I presented my plan to Mai and Ty Lee. "We have been given an extraordinary opportunity, girls. The chance to conquer Ba Sing Se."

I can see that I have shocked them. They are loyal companions and fine soldiers, but they lack any capacity for thinking beyond what is right before their faces.

"I thought we just wanted to capture the Avatar," Mai replied.

"Why settle for the Avatar when we can have the whole Earth Kingdom? For one hundred years we have tried to break into Ba Sing Se from the outside. But now we are here, inside, and we can take the city by ourselves."

Still they stare at me like wide-eyed deer. Looks like I will have to spell it out for them. "We have the king's trust, and so we are in a perfect position to organize a coup and overthrow him," I explained. "The key is the Dai Li. Whoever controls the Dai Li controls Ba Sing Se."

And I intend to control the Dai Li—without them even knowing it. First I have to get them to believe that they have the upper hand. I have spotted them spying on us as we moved about the city, although they are, of course, unaware that I know of their presence. A well-timed, well-rehearsed conversation for them to overhear our "plans" should plant the proper seed.

The following day I sent Mai and Ty Lee outside the palace while I waited just inside the doorway.

"How much longer do we have to serve the Earth King?" Mai asked.

"Princess Azula promised we would go back to the Fire Nation once we capture the Avatar."

"Shhh! Do you want the whole palace to know we're Fire Nation?"

I laughed to myself and was proud of the girls. The bait has been cast, and I'm certain the fish have bitten. Now to add a final convincing touch: I stepped into the palace with an angry look on my face, as if I'd just overheard their blunder. Mai and Ty Lee looked sufficiently ashamed. After a few minutes, when I was sure the Dai Li spies had scampered back into their holes to report this terribly interesting piece of news to their leaders, I dismissed Mai and Ty Lee. "Good work, girls," I said.

That night, still dressed as Kyoshi warriors, we returned to the king's throne room to continue the pretense of being his loyal servants. But the king was not there. And then another gift was handed to us.

The Waterbender who travels with the Avatar burst into the throne room. We retreated to the shadows, preparing for a fight, but the girl mistook us for real Kyoshi warriors, including one she obviously knew by name.

"Suki! It's Katara. Something terrible is going on," she cried. "The Fire Nation has infiltrated the city!"

72

How could word of our presence have traveled so fast that Katara is aware of it? And why would the Dai Li share information like that with her?

"I just saw Prince Zuko and his uncle!" she continued.

So THAT is what she means. I am relieved that she is unaware of our true identities, and very, very intrigued that Zu–zu is in the city. Things keep falling into place with each passing day. This scheme is indeed my masterstroke, destined to place me in Father's good graces forever.

"We have to tell the Earth King right away!" exclaimed Katara.

Oh, really? Well. I don't need to maintain this masquerade any longer. You are no match for the three of us, Waterbender. I stepped out from the shadows. "Oh, don't worry. I'll be sure to tell him."

Shocked, Katara pulled water from her pouch, but before she could bend it in an attack, Ty Lee was on her, blocking her chi. The water splashed harmlessly to the ground, then the girl crumpled into a heap at my feet. "Take her to the prison," I told the girls.

Katara will no longer trouble us, but I can't stop thinking about my brother. "I think it's time for a family reunion," I said as the girls left the room.

That night, before I had a chance to search for Zuko, several Dai Li agents slipped into my room and hurried me to the palace prison. I had been expecting something like this, and had instructed Mai and Ty Lee not to interfere. Now I must give the Dai Li the impression that I am outraged, and that I have no idea that they know exactly who I am.

The Dai Li brought me to Long Feng's cell. "What is this about?" I shouted, trying to sound as indignant as possible. "Your agents drag me down here in the middle of the night? You will not treat a Kyoshi warrior this way!"

"But you are not a Kyoshi warrior, are you, Princess Azula of the Fire Nation?" Long Feng replied with a smirk.

I flashed him my most convincing look of shock and dismay. "What do you want?" I asked.

I listened as he proposed a deal. He wanted to take back control of Ba Sing Se and he told me that I had something that he needed—the Earth King's trust.

"Why should I help you?" I asked. Come on, take the bait, step into my trap.

"Because I can get you the Avatar."

Perfect! He thinks he has me. "I'm listening."

I stood there and pretended to be interested in his plan to capture the Avatar and deliver him to the Fire Nation. I don't know if he's lying or not, but it really doesn't matter. Whatever he thinks he will do is incorrect: In the end he will do exactly as I want. So for now, I tell him that we have a deal. The look of satisfaction on the pathetic man's face is sickening.

As I head back to my chambers, I remind myself that it won't be long before Long Feng realizes how stupid he really is. All the wheels are in motion. Now we just have to put together the final pieces of my plan.

降击神通

Chapter 6

Even though I was nervous, I was not about to show it in front of the group of Dai Li agents I had gathered. Everything hinges on the performance I am about to give. I need their trust, but if I can't have that, I need to inspire fear. I have found that fear is a stronger motivator than trust, especially among those, like the Dai Li, who are used to operating along the shadowy edges of the rules.

"The Earth King and the Council of Generals do not trust the Dai Li," I said firmly.

"They imprisoned your leader, Long Feng. Next they will eliminate you. We must seize power at once. Our coup must be swift and decisive. The king and his generals must be taken out simultaneously. Then the military will fall under our control."

I have captured their attention. Now this is it, the moment in which I establish control. I really have to sell this.

"Long Feng has placed you in MY command while we overthrow the government. For some of you, it might be difficult and strange to ally yourself with a Fire Nation princess. But you must banish that prejudice from your heart."

I believe that if I make an example of one agent, the others will follow. Yes, this one looks suitably nervous. I'll stare at him directly in the eyes as I deliver the final piece.

"If I sense any disloyalty, any hesitation, any weakness at all . . . I will snuff it out!"

The agent bowed to me, refusing to stand back up until I had spoken. It couldn't have been more perfect. They are all now my servants. "That is all," I said dismissively.

The Dai Li hurried from the room, leaving only Ty Lee and Mai at my side.

"Nice speech, Azula!" Ty Lee said. "Pretty and poetic, but also scary, in a good way."

Precisely my intention. "I thought it went well," I replied. "But there are still a few loose ends—the Avatar, and my brother and uncle."

I sent a message to Iroh's tea shop—making it look as if the note had come from the Earth King—requesting that he and Zuko come to the palace as guests of the king, to personally serve him tea. There was no way Iroh could resist such an offer.

The next day, I watched from the shadows as Iroh and Zuko set up tea in the palace tea room.

I marveled at how soft and so pitifully domesticated they had both become. The once great general, who was called the Dragon of the West, and the Fire Lord's firstborn, preparing tea like servants. If my father could see his son . . . Well, no matter. Soon they will be back in the Fire Nation, or else they will be destroyed.

At a signal from me, the Dai Li agents entered the room.

"Something's not right," Zuko said, noticing their presence.

Smart boy. Something is most definitely not right . . . for you!

"It's teatime!" I announced as I stepped out of the shadows.

"Azula!" Zuko cried.

I could see the fear in his eyes. Still, he put on a brave face, stepping toward me as if he was ready to fight. A Dai Li agent quickly stepped into Zuko's path.

The loyalty of the Dai Li is without question. They are willing to lay down their lives to protect me. Excellent. This unwavering allegiance will be necessary in order to complete my ascent to the throne.

Iroh calmly sipped his tea. He is better at not showing panic than Zu-zu. "Did I ever tell you how I got the nickname Dragon of the West?" he asked.

I don't know which is worse: fighting Iroh, or being bored to death by one of his hopelessly longwinded stories. "I'm not interested in a lengthy anecdote, Uncle," I said impatiently.

"It's more of a demonstration, really," Iroh insisted.

Then he suddenly Firebended a blazing burst of flame from his mouth. The Dai Li scattered in all directions, and Iroh and Zuko ran from the tea room. The Dai Li and I chased them down the hall—and into a hallway that was a dead end. They were trapped!

But then Iroh did something that surprised me: He used a lightning attack to blast a hole in the wall and jumped several stories down to the ground.

"Come on, Zuko," he called from below.

"No," Zuko said firmly. "I'm tired of running. It's time I faced Azula."

"You're so dramatic, Brother," I said. "Are you challenging me?"

Zuko glowered. "Yes, I challenge you."

"No thanks," I replied, just as Zuko unleashed a powerful Firebending attack that was easily blocked by the Dai Li agents. They Earthbended a huge wall of rock to deflect the flames. Then the agents swarmed on Zuko, quickly subduing him.

Seeing this made me realize that as much as I enjoy a good fight, I could get used to having a squadron of agents handling my enemies for me every now and then!

The rest of my plan was quickly set in motion. With Katara and Zuko locked away in an underground prison chamber, I set the Dai Li to the task of arresting and imprisoning all the generals on the Council of Generals.

At long last, I will soon sit upon the throne of the Earth Kingdom.

🀄 🀄 🀄

We returned to the king's throne room, and this time he was there. Mai and Ty Lee took up their bodyguard positions on either side of the throne, and I once again lingered in the shadows.

A short while later, the other two members of the Avatar's party—the tall warrior boy and the Earthbending girl—rushed into the throne room. As the two approached the king, Ty Lee and Mai attacked. The Earthbender managed to put Mai on the defensive while the boy was able to avoid Ty Lee's chi—blocking moves.

Very skillful. But I have the upper hand in these matters. Now that the king knows that we are not really Kyoshi warriors, I can finally drop this annoying pretense. I stepped up to the king and placed my hand beside his head, preparing to strike him with a Firebending blow. I felt him stiffen with fear.

"This fight is over," I said.

The boy and the Earthbender stopped, seeing that the Earth King was in serious danger. "Get them out of my sight," I ordered. Mai, Ty Lee, and two Dai Li agents hauled everyone—including the Earth King—off to the prison.

I stood alone in the throne room—MY throne room, now that our little charade had ended. I'm going to like it here as ruler of the Earth Kingdom.

Then Long Feng walked in, surrounded by a throng of Dai Li agents. There was just one more step on my road to the throne: Long Feng was the final obstacle on my journey.

"It looks like the coup has gone perfectly," he said.

"It has," I responded.

"Now comes the part where I double-cross you, Azula. Dai Li, arrest the Fire Nation princess!"

Nobody moved. The Dai Li stood their ground. Ha! Long Feng, you are a fool. These men are smart enough to know that betraying me would have far more severe consequences than would turning their backs on you.

"They haven't made up their minds," I said, pleased with the agents' loyalty. "They're going to wait to see how this ends. To learn who will sit on the throne. They are not sure which one of us will bow down. But I know—and so do you, Long Feng."

I strode slowly to the throne and sat down as if I had always been in that seat. I stared at Long Feng, letting him think everything over. There is only one conclusion he can come to. Only one choice for him to make. And he knows it. He heaved a heavy sigh, then bowed to me.

"You've beaten me at my own game," he said heavily.

Don't flatter yourself, Long Feng. You were my pawn from the beginning. It's too bad that you've only now realized the extent of my power.

"You were never even a player," I said. Then I nodded to the Dai Li, who swooped down on Long Feng and took him to the prison.

Finally alone in my throne room, I took a moment to savor being ruler of the Earth Kingdom. Not bad for a fourteen-year-old.

But I still had to prepare myself to deal with Zuko.

I took a squad of Dai Li agents with me and headed for the prison chambers in the underground crystal catacombs. There, I overheard Iroh trying to convince Zuko to forsake his heritage, to turn his back on his destiny, and to oppose me.

When I reached their chamber, I immediately ordered the Dai Li to Earthbend a crystal cave around Iroh, so he couldn't help his nephew. Then I turned to face Zuko.

"I expected this kind of treachery from Uncle, but you, Prince Zuko, are no traitor. Are you? It's not too late, Zuko. You can still redeem yourself."

I know he doesn't believe Iroh and all his talk of turning to goodness. I know what Zuko wants deep in his heart. I have always known him better than anyone else. He can't hide his true feelings and desires from me, no matter what he says, no matter how noble a face he puts on for others. I know what choice he will make, even if he doesn't know.

Iroh had tried to persuade him not to join me, but I told Zuko that we needed to work as a team, to share in the conquest of Ba Sing Se, and to complete the Fire Nation's world domination together. What was more, I reminded him, was that he could restore his honor, capture the Avatar, and reclaim our father's love.

"You will have everything you want if you join me," I said patiently. "You are free to choose." Then I ordered the Dai Li to release him, sure of what his decision would be.

I must now turn my attention to the Avatar.

I caught up with him in the crystal courtyard—and he was with Katara! The Avatar must have released her from prison. I fired blasts of blue lightning that shot through the crystal walls, but Katara sent a sheet of ice beneath my feet. Then the Avatar Earthbended a rock ledge that knocked me down.

These two are proving to be worthwhile opponents.

We battled on until a huge red fireball suddenly exploded in the center of the courtyard. Zuko! For a split second I had a moment of doubt. Could I have been wrong, and he was attacking ME? It didn't take Zuko long to answer my question. He turned and released a barrage of fire—right at the Avatar.

My dear brother, you were born to be a prince of the Fire Nation, and now the time has come for you to fulfill that destiny by my side. Together we battled the Avatar and the Waterbender, who tried to make Zuko feel guilty about his choice. He hesitated for a moment, poor, weak Zu-zu, but then fired a blast at Katara.

She stumbled back into a stream. This is my chance! I fired a charge of lightning into the stream. It traveled through the water and struck Katara. She collapsed from the shock.

Then something unexpected happened. The Avatar's tattoos began to glow, and he seemed to grow in power—but he also appeared to be distracted by this strange state he had entered.

Now it ends, Avatar! I blasted him from behind with my most powerful lightning bolt. His tattoos stopped glowing and he crumpled to the ground. At the same time, Katara recovered. She quickly rushed to his side, but this fight was over.

Zuko and I approached the weakened girl and the motionless Avatar, and prepared for our final victory.

Suddenly a rush of fire and lightning filled the air, blocking our path to the helpless duo.

Iroh! The traitor has managed to free

himself. But he cannot take away my ultimate moment of glory. I will not allow it.

Although I defeated Iroh, he fought fiercely. By the time I was able to subdue him, Katara—and more important, the Avatar—had vanished.

And so the Avatar has escaped yet again. But unlike the other times, I am less upset about it, as I now have two great victories to celebrate.

I returned to the throne room and sat on my new throne, with Zuko standing beside me. "We've done it, Zuko. It's taken one hundred years, but thanks to us, the Fire Nation has conquered Ba Sing Se."

Zuko, however, was not in such a joyous mood. He falls back so easily into his moody, brooding habits. "I betrayed Uncle," he said, with shame in his voice.

"No, Brother, he betrayed you," I said. "When you return home, Father will welcome you as a war hero."

"But I don't have the Avatar. What if Father doesn't restore my honor?" he asked.

Poor, poor Zuko. I actually feel sorry for

him. He still doesn't understand, even at his moment of ultimate achievement.

"Father doesn't need to restore your honor, Zuko," I explained. "Today you restored your own honor."

My brother looked away from me with a pained expression across his face. I hope he can eventually believe what I have told him: that by choosing his family, by choosing me over the Avatar, he has come back to his rightful place in the Fire Nation.

And I welcome him by my side.

DON'T MISS

THE EARTH KINGDOM CHRONICLES:
THE TALE OF
AANG

READ A CHAPTER FROM
THE BOOK NOW!

We flew over the Earth Kingdom, not sure where we were headed next. As we passed over a swamp, I heard it calling to me, telling me to land. I figured if I was actually hearing the Earth, I probably shouldn't ignore it.

A few seconds later, a fierce wind pulled us down toward the swamp. By the time we landed, we had all gotten separated. While I was on my own, I had this vision of a laughing girl in a white dress. She seemed to want me to follow her, and she just kept laughing as I chased her through the swamp. Then she disappeared.

The wind turned out to just be a Water-bender who was trying to protect the swamp. He told us that the swamp is actually just one giant tree that is connected to everything, that the entire world is connected, and that time is an illusion.

But if time really is an illusion, maybe the girl I saw is someone I will meet in the future. Sokka and Katara also had visions, only theirs were of people from their past. Hmm . . . sometimes I wish I were just plain smarter. It would sure come in handy as the Avatar!

⊕ ⊕ ⊕

Anyway, we left the swamp and went to the town of Gaoling to Master Yu's Earthbending Academy in search of a teacher. But all Master Yu did was try to sell me more lessons. That's when I realized he's definitely not the one!

Then I heard about an Earthbending tournament called Earth Rumble Six, where the top Earthbenders in town competed against one another. So we went to watch. It was like nothing I'd ever seen! Xin Fu, who was running it, kept introducing Earthbenders with names like the Boulder and the Gopher. Boy, were they huge! The Boulder had beaten everyone in sight so far! At first I thought the Boulder was the champion, but I really couldn't see him being the teacher Bumi was talking about. I'm pretty sure the Boulder doesn't ever wait or listen. Oh, here comes the Boulder's final opponent—she's a twelve-year-old blind girl! She calls herself the Blind Bandit. SHE'S actually the reigning champion. She must be incredible. I can't wait to watch her!

Just then the Blind Bandit began to laugh defiantly.

Wait a second—I've heard that laugh before! She's the girl from my vision in the swamp! The vision really was of someone from the future. I guess I'm pretty smart after all!

Then the most incredible thing yet happened—the Blind Bandit beat the Boulder! Every time the Boulder took a step, the Blind Bandit knew exactly where he was. She shifted her weight from one foot to the other. The small movement was power-ful enough to create a ripple in the ground, which rushed toward the Boulder like a wave. As he put his foot down, the wave struck it, causing him to hit the ground with his legs split wide apart. Then the Blind Bandit forced three stone spikes to burst from the ground, slamming into the Boulder and knocking him from the ring. The match was over in a mat-ter of seconds.

"Winner and still champion, the Blind Bandit!" Xin Fu shouted from the center of the arena.

"How did she do that?" Katara asked.

The answer struck me at once. "She waited, and she listened." Just like Bumi said.

Then the announcer offered gold to any—one from the audience who could beat her, and I volunteered. I just wanted to get close enough to ask her to be my Earthbending teacher, but she kept knocking me with Earthbending moves. Finally I had to knock her down with an Airbending blow. She was pretty angry and stormed out of the arena.

We finally tracked her down as a member of the Beifong family. She's royalty! Pretty strange, huh? Anyway, we traveled to the house of Lao and Poppy Beifong. What a mansion! It's on a huge estate with gardens, servants, and everything. I announced myself as the Avatar, and Katara, Sokka, and I were invited in for dinner. At the dinner table sat the Blind Bandit, whose real name is Toph Beifong. Master Yu, the head of the Earthbending Academy, was there too. He's Toph's Earthbending teacher—like she needs one!

Anyway, it turned out that her parents didn't have a clue how powerful an Earthbender she is. They still thought she was a beginner! After dinner she told me that even though her parents saw her blindness as a handicap and were more protective of her because of it, she's always been able to see by using her Earthbending. She feels vibrations through her feet and that tells her everything she needs to know—and way more than most of us can see.

In the end, she had to tell her parents the truth because we were ambushed by the Earthbenders from Earth Rumble Six—they wanted to steal back the gold I had won. It all worked out though, and Toph agreed to be my teacher! I'm so excited. I think she's going to be exactly the teacher that Bumi wanted me to have.

We're off on Appa, again, and for the first time in a while, things are finally starting to look up.